Dear Parent,

"How come I'm always last?"

How many times have you heard that from your child?

Now here's a delightful tale about a sad little puppy who's always last—until one day . . .

Using simple illustrations and easy-to-read words to tell this humorous tale, Frank Asch, one of America's most beloved illustrators for children, creates a story every youngster can relate to.

As you follow the misadventures of the little puppy, your child will learn—as the puppy eventually does—that good things really do come to those who wait!

Take a few minutes now to share this story with your child. I know it's one you'll both enjoy together.

Sincerely,

Elizabeth Isele
Executive Editor
Weekly Reader Books

Weekly Reader Children's Book Club Presents

The Last Puppy

FRANK ASCH

Simon and Schuster Books for Young Readers
Published by Simon & Schuster Inc., New York

To Winnie and Gesso

the last to learn to drink milk
from a saucer,

and the last one into the doghouse
at night.

I was the last of Momma's nine puppies.

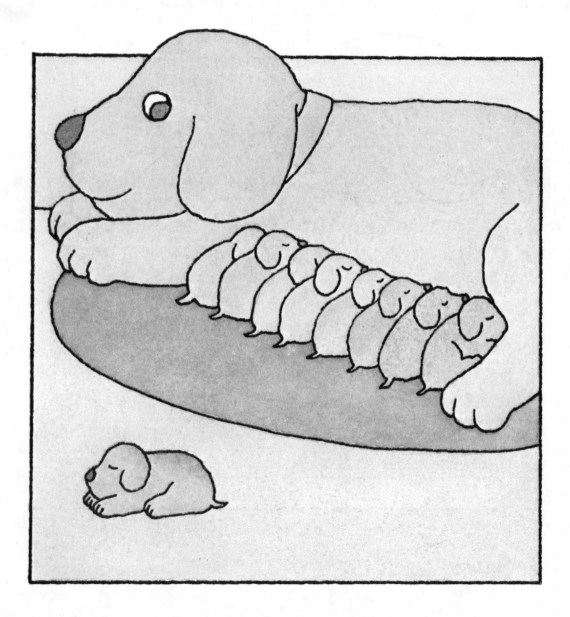

The last to eat from Momma,
the last to open my eyes,

I was the last puppy.

One day Momma's owner put up a sign:
PUPPIES FOR SALE.

The next day, a little girl came
and took one of us away.
That night I couldn't sleep very well.
I kept wondering:
When will my turn come?
Will I be the last puppy again?

In the morning, a little boy
came to choose a puppy.
"Take me, Take me!" I barked.
"That puppy's too noisy," he said,
and picked another puppy instead.

Later that day, a nice lady from
the city almost picked me.
But when I tried to jump into
her lap, she fell backwards
right into our bowl of milk.

When a farmer and his family
came to choose a puppy,
I got so excited when
the farmer picked me up,
I bit him on the nose.
They picked two puppies,
leaving four of us behind.

Soon there were just three of us left.

Then two,

then just me, the last puppy.

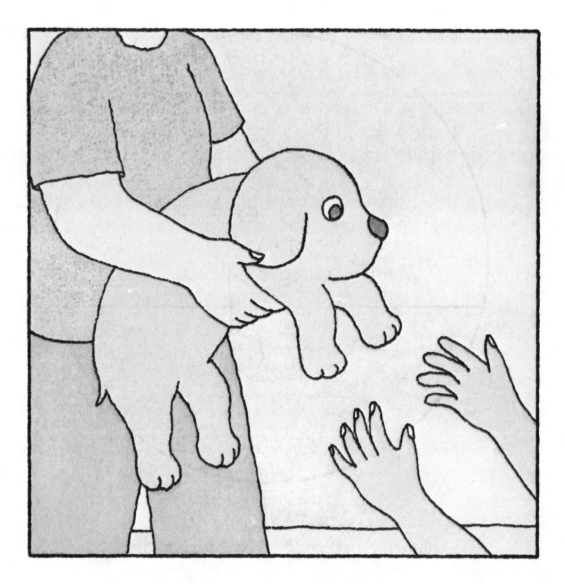

Later that day, a nice lady from
the city almost picked me.
But when I tried to jump into
her lap, she fell backwards
right into our bowl of milk.

But one day, my turn came, too.
Big hands picked me up
and gave me to a little boy.
We got into a car
and drove away.

The little boy held me on his lap.
He put his face down close to mine
and I licked him on the nose.

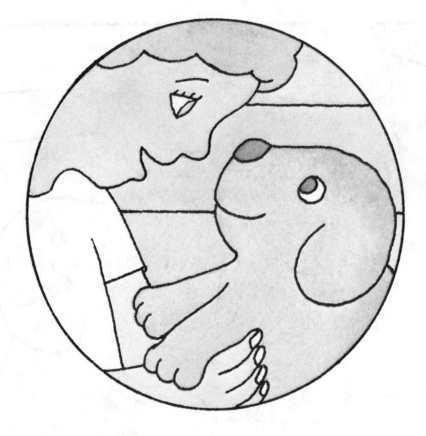

He laughed and said,
"You know what?
You're my first puppy."